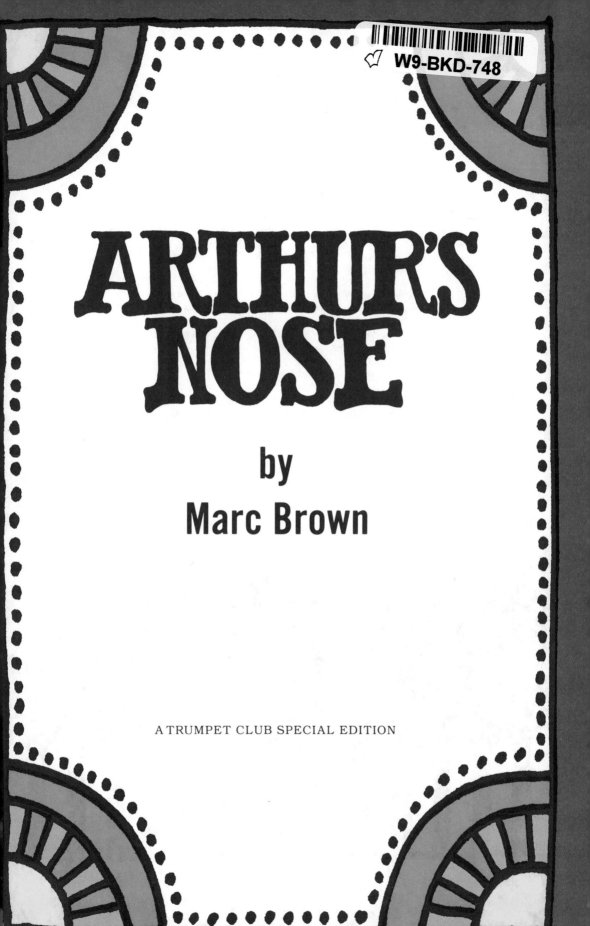

# ARTHUR'S NOSE

by

## Marc Brown

*ISBN 0-590-16218-7*

*Copyright © 1976 by Marc Brown.
All rights reserved. Published by Scholastic Inc., 555 Broadway,
New York, NY 10012, by arrangement with Little, Brown and Company (Inc.).
TRUMPET and the TRUMPET logo are registered trademarks
of Scholastic Inc.*

*12  11*                                                              *9/9  0  1/0*

                                                                         *09*

*Printed in the U.S.A.*

This is Arthur's house.

This is Arthur.
He is worried
about his nose.

This is Arthur's mom.

This is Arthur's dad.

This is Arthur's sister.

They all love Arthur, and they all like his nose.

One day Arthur decided he didn't like his nose.
He had a cold and his nose was red.
His sister thought his nose looked funny.

His nose was a nuisance at school.
Francine, who sat in front of Arthur, complained to the teacher that Arthur's nose was always bothering her.

When Arthur played hide-and-seek,
friends always found him first.

His friends thought his nose was funny.
But what could he do about it?

He could change his nose!
That's what he could
do about it.

Arthur told his friends that he was going
to the rhinologist for a new nose.
His friends were very surprised.

Doctor Louise was very helpful. She suggested that Arthur try on pictures of different noses. That way he could choose the one he liked best.

# Arthur tried on all kinds of noses.

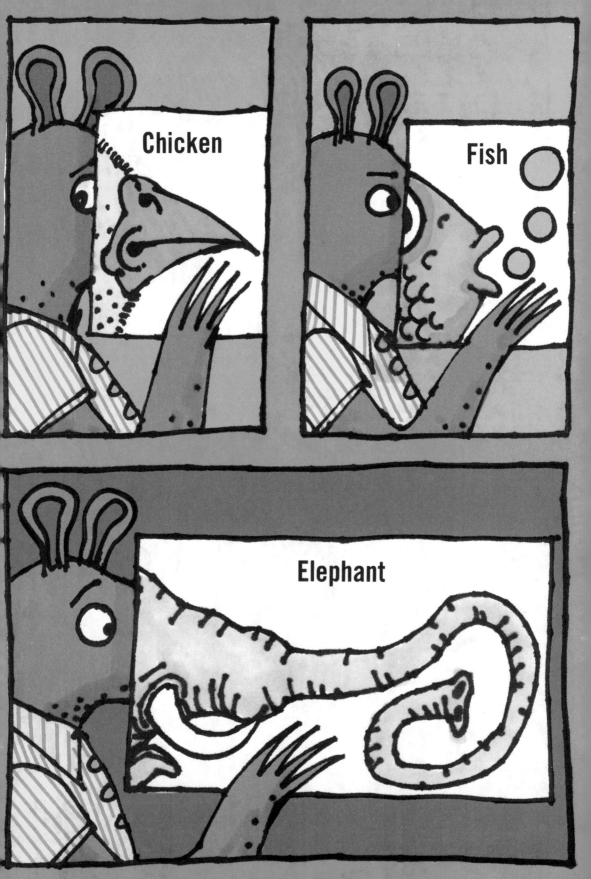

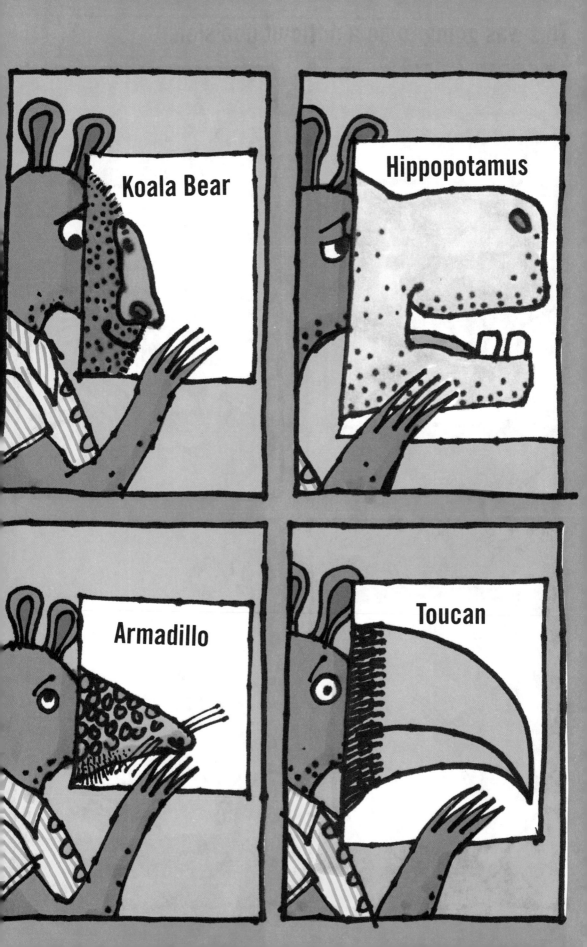

# This was going to be a difficult decision.

Arthur's friends waited outside
to see which nose he would choose.

Arthur hadn't changed his nose at all.

"I tried on every nose there was.
I'm just not me without my nose!"
said Arthur.

It's a nice nose.

There's a lot more to Arthur than his nose.

Ms. Yollanda
Grade 1